The Impeachment of President Donald Trump

John Allen

ReferencePoint
Press

San Diego, CA

© 2021 ReferencePoint Press, Inc.
Printed in the United States

For more information, contact:
ReferencePoint Press, Inc.
PO Box 27779
San Diego, CA 92198
www.ReferencePointPress.com

LIBRARY OF CONGRESS CATALOGING-IN-PUBLICATION DATA

Names: Allen, John, 1957- editor.
Title: The impeachment of President Donald Trump
Description: San Diego, CA : ReferencePoint Press, Inc., 2020. | Includes
   bibliographical references and index.
Identifiers: LCCN 2020019537 (print) | LCCN 2020019538 (ebook) | ISBN
   9781682829011 (library binding) | ISBN 9781682829028 (ebook)
Subjects: LCSH: Trump, Donald, 1946---Impeachment--Juvenile literature. |
   Impeachments--United States--Juvenile literature.
Classification: LCC KF5076.T78 I47 2020 (print) | LCC KF5076.T78 (ebook)
   | DDC 342.73/062--dc23
LC record available at https://lccn.loc.gov/2020019537
LC ebook record available at https://lccn.loc.gov/2020019538

Contents

A Phone Call Sets Off a Firestorm

On July 25, 2019, President Donald Trump had a phone conversation with Volodymyr Zelensky, the newly elected president of Ukraine. The purpose of the call was to congratulate Zelensky on his recent election victory. At one point during the call—according to a transcript-like summary compiled from notes and recollections by US officials listening in—Trump asked Zelensky for a favor. He wanted the Ukrainian government to investigate former vice president Joe Biden and his son Hunter; the latter served on the board of a Ukrainian energy company. Joe Biden was considered the frontrunner to win the Democratic Party's nomination for president in 2020.

Early in September, an anonymous intelligence official filed a whistleblower complaint against Trump. The whistleblower wrote, "In the course of my official duties, I have received information from multiple U.S. Government officials that the President of the United States is using the power of his office to solicit interference from a foreign country in the 2020 U.S. election."[1] Trump was accused of withholding nearly $400 million in military aid to Ukraine in order to pressure Zelensky to investigate the Bidens. In response to the complaint, the White House released the rough transcript of the call. Trump claimed it showed he had done nothing wrong.

He later described his conversation with the Ukrainian president as "perfect."[2] However, the revelation that he did indeed press Zelensky to probe his political rival set off a firestorm in the media and across the nation. On September 24, 2019, House Speaker Nancy Pelosi announced an inquiry that would eventually lead to the impeachment of the president of the United States.

A Series of Investigations

The move to impeach Trump was the latest in a series of investigations of the president, some dating to before he took office. The Ukraine controversy erupted not long after Trump had escaped the most serious threat to his presidency. Special Prosecutor Robert Mueller and his team had looked into Russian interference in the 2016 presidential campaign along with charges that Trump had conspired with Russia to steal the election. The investigation lasted nearly two years and brought thirty-seven indictments, including five against Trump associates and campaign members. Mueller found that Russia had engaged in numerous systematic efforts to interfere in the 2016 election. However, Mueller's team found insufficient evidence of a conspiracy. His final report, released to the public on April 18, 2019, was critical of Trump and his associates and left open the question of whether Trump had obstructed justice. Nonetheless, Trump claimed he was cleared of any wrongdoing. He also dismissed the Mueller probe as a partisan witch hunt.

> "In the course of my official duties, I have received information from multiple U.S. Government officials that the President of the United States is using the power of his office to solicit interference from a foreign country in the 2020 U.S. election."[1]
>
> —A whistleblower in the US intelligence service

It was not long before the Trump White House was embroiled in another crisis. The Ukraine controversy erupted only a few months after the release of the Mueller report. In fact, the Zelensky call took place one day after Mueller testified to Congress about his team's findings. By September, the media were again questioning whether Trump could survive in office. Observers noted that the whistleblower's accusations resembled those made earlier in connection with Russian election interference. Once more the president stood accused of seeking election interference from a foreign country.

An Administration Marked by Chaos and Conflict

With his background as a billionaire celebrity, real estate mogul, and reality television star, Trump has been utterly unlike any other modern president. His startling victory over Democrat Hillary Clinton in the 2016 election caught experts off guard. Trump's lack of governing experience led to predictions of disaster. His belligerence toward America's allies and rejection of longtime trade pacts alarmed his critics. They claimed his stance of "America First" reeked of nationalism. His crusade to build a border wall to stop illegal immigration from Mexico and Central America was widely called racist. Accusations that he had mistreated women in the

President Donald Trump meets with Ukrainian president Volodymyr Zelensky in New York in September 2019. A phone call between the two men just a couple of months earlier led to Trump's impeachment.

past refused to go away in the age of #MeToo. What especially outraged Trump's opponents was his flouting of rules regarding presidential conduct. He gave his rivals insulting nicknames and issued a flood of tweets on whatever subject struck his fancy. He particularly enjoyed attacking some of the nation's most respected media outlets for what he repeatedly described as their lies and fake news reporting.

From the start, Trump's administration was marked by chaos and conflict. As president, Trump demanded absolute loyalty from those around him. Disagreement often resulted in dismissal. Everyone from the White House chief of staff to cabinet members were prey to Trump's whims and tantrums. Fired officials wrote memoirs about the difficulty of working with such an unpredictable president. Yet despite the turmoil, Trump achieved success in some areas. In the first three years of his presidency, the US economy gained strength, and employment numbers soared, especially for minorities. Polls showed that a majority of Americans disapproved of Trump but liked certain of his policies.

Raising Fundamental Questions

The Trump impeachment saga raised important questions about American government. It sparked debates about what acts are impeachable and the limits of presidential power. It also highlighted the tense relationship between Trump and the administrative state—what Trump and his allies call the "deep state," or permanent bureaucracy. Trump has repeatedly questioned the work of US intelligence agencies. He disputed findings that Russia hacked the servers of the Democratic National Committee and tried to influence the election. Trump's defenders saw the whistleblower complaint as the deep state's latest attempt to undo the 2016 election and remove him from office. Whatever the truth of such claims, Americans remain deeply divided on the Trump impeachment. And the controversy surrounding Trump's presidency shows no sign of going away.

What Is Impeachment?

Impeachment is a process through which the president and other federal officials, including judges, can be held accountable for their actions. In the case of the president, Congress conducts the impeachment proceedings. As laid out in the US Constitution, impeachment is a political process, not a criminal process. The process requires actions by both the House of Representatives and the Senate. In the case of a presidential impeachment, the House brings charges against the president for misconduct or wrongdoing. Impeachment in the House does not involve actually removing the president from office. That step must be taken by the Senate.

Impeachment starts in the House of Representatives, where the process can be launched at the request of any House member. The Speaker of the House, acting as leader of the majority party, must decide whether to go forward with an inquiry, or investigation, into the alleged presidential wrongdoing.

The Constitution lists "treason, bribery, or other high crimes and misdemeanors" as offenses that deserve impeachment. Experts have long debated what behavior could be considered "high crimes and misdemeanors." Most legal experts insist that a president need not have committed an actual crime in order to be impeached. For example, a president may be impeached for some form of abuse of power.

A simple majority vote by the members of the House Judiciary Committee is required to send each article of impeachment to the full House. Then it takes a simple majority vote of the full House to impeach the president, or affirm the articles against him or her.

Once the president has been impeached by the House, the process moves to the Senate for a trial on the impeachment. The Constitution allows the leader of the Senate and the majority party to set the rules of the trial. The chief justice of the United States presides over the trial.

For the president to be removed, two-thirds of the Senate must approve. That means that at least sixty-seven senators must vote for removal. This vote only removes the sitting president from office; it does not send the president to jail. If a president is removed, the vice president takes over as president.

Chapter One

The Whistleblower's Complaint

In his job as inspector general for the US intelligence community, Michael Atkinson was used to handling the most sensitive matters. He looked into possible violations of laws, rules, and regulations related to national intelligence. On August 26, 2019, he weighed in on a complaint by an anonymous whistleblower, one he realized could be fatal to the presidency of Donald Trump. In a letter to Joseph Maguire, the acting Director of National Intelligence (DNI), Atkinson expressed his belief that the complaint was an "urgent concern"[3] that appeared to be credible. He noted that, under the law, Maguire had one week to forward the complaint to lawmakers in the House.

Despite Atkinson's recommendation, by September 9 Maguire still had not contacted Congress. Maguire disagreed that the allegations rose to the level of an urgent concern. It was left to Atkinson to notify the House intelligence committee about the whistleblower's complaint. Three House committees immediately announced a probe into Trump's alleged efforts to pressure Ukraine for his political benefit, and thus began the months-long investigation that would lead to Trump's impeachment.

A Credible Allegation

By the time Congress received Atkinson's letter, a few facts about Trump's phone call had already been made public. Reports citing anonymous sources revealed that the president had urged Zelensky to investigate Democrat Joe Biden's son Hunter. The leaked reports also suggested that Trump threatened to withhold military aid to Ukraine if Zelensky did not cooperate. Republicans mostly dismissed the stories as partisan rumor. However, when the inspector general's opinion about the complaint emerged, the tone changed. Atkinson's solid reputation convinced many skeptical Republicans that the matter was serious. The Trump appointee was widely considered an honest and forthright professional. "You would not know which political party [Atkinson] favors by working with him," says Mary McCord, the former assistant attorney general for national security. "I worked with him for years. That's the other reason I feel he's so credible in this space."[4]

Michael Atkinson, inspector general for the US intelligence community, arrives at the Capitol in October 2019 to speak with lawmakers about the whistleblower complaint that he earlier had determined was both urgent and credible.

With Acting DNI Maguire still opposed, Atkinson was not authorized to go into detail about the whistleblower's concerns. All he could do was make lawmakers aware of the complaint. In a closed-door appearance on September 19, 2019, Atkinson told the House Intelligence Committee that he and Maguire remained at an impasse. Yet Atkinson's decision to go over Maguire's head and alert members of Congress about the complaint proved crucial. His insistence that the whistleblower's allegation was credible set in motion powerful forces that soon would threaten Trump's presidency.

A Grilling Before the Intelligence Committee

By September 26, when Maguire appeared before the House Intelligence Committee, the whistleblower story had exploded. Characteristically, the president disavowed any problems.

When reporters asked Trump if he had read the whistleblower's complaint, he ridiculed the media response. "Everybody has read it and they laugh at it," he said. "The media has lost so much credibility in this country. Our media has become the laughingstock of the world."[5] Nonetheless, to most of official Washington, the complaint was no laughing matter.

> "Everybody has read it and they laugh at it. The media has lost so much credibility in this country. Our media has become the laughingstock of the world."[5]
>
> —President Trump on the whistleblower complaint

Sparks flew as members of the House Intelligence Committee grilled Maguire about his decision to withhold the whistleblower report from Congress. Maguire, who had been serving as the DNI for only a few weeks, repeatedly defended his actions by saying the situation was unprecedented. All previous whistleblower complaints to the DNI had flagged members of the intelligence community, not the president. He also raised questions of executive privilege. This is the rule whereby sensitive documents or information related to the president and members of the executive branch can be shielded from release.

However, Chairman Adam Schiff and his fellow Democrats on the committee slammed Maguire for what they considered possible legal violations. They noted that whistleblower complaints are protected by law. "Regardless of whether it's found credible or incredible, you're aware the complaint is always given to our committee,"[6] said Schiff. Maguire also admitted that he had spoken to Trump about the report but said the president had not directed him to withhold anything. Overall, Maguire's six hours of testimony seemed only to increase the heat on Trump and his inner circle. The hearing, along with the release of the phone conversation, helped push the impeachment investigation into high gear.

Focusing on the Whistleblower

Suddenly, the hot topic nationwide was the anonymous whistleblower. A whistleblower is someone who informs on a person or group allegedly engaged in illicit activity. The Whistleblower Protection Act of 1989 offers certain protections to informers in the federal government. For example, they cannot be demoted, replaced, or punished with pay cuts. These protections are designed to encourage government officials to speak out about misconduct they have witnessed without fear of reprisal. The statute, as applied to the Trump whistleblower, prohibited national intelligence officials from naming the person or describing his or her position. It also laid out the proper procedures for reviewing the complaint. During his House testimony, Maguire stressed that protecting the whistleblower was the highest priority of his office.

Naturally, a great deal of curiosity arose about the whistleblower. People wanted to know what position the person held and how he or she came to discover the alleged abuses. Schiff and other Democrats said they were anxious to hear from the whistleblower. Such testimony would have required a closed ses-

The Ukraine Connection

When the controversy over President Trump's phone call with the Ukrainian president broke out, many Americans might have struggled to find Ukraine on a map. It is a large country located in eastern Europe on the Black Sea. Formerly part of the Soviet Union, Ukraine became an independent country in 1991 after the Soviet collapse. Although Ukraine's history is closely linked with Russia's, the country has its own language and distinct culture. Tensions with Russia have marked the history of Ukraine for decades, even centuries.

In recent years, the United States and the European Union have urged Ukraine to develop closer ties with the West. Russian president Vladimir Putin has worked hard to block these efforts. In 2014, widespread protests in Ukraine led to the ouster of its pro-Russian president Victor Yanukovych. When Yanukovych was replaced with an interim government that was pro-Western, Putin sent Russian troops into Ukraine. The troops helped pro-Russian separatists to seize Crimea, a sizable region in southern Ukraine. The world community, including the United States, condemned the move as a violation of international law. US intelligence agencies urged President Barack Obama to support Ukraine against Russian aggression. Obama sent nonlethal military aid—equipment and medical supplies—to Ukraine in 2015. He also sent American troops to train Ukraine's forces. However, a bipartisan majority in Congress wanted to provide more weapons to the beleaguered regime. In 2019, Congress passed a $391 billion military package for Ukraine's defense—the spending package that Trump was thought to have withheld.

sion to protect the whistleblower's identity along with special security clearances for the individual's attorneys. Republicans such as Representative Andy Harris of Maryland, questioned whether the whistleblower's complaint might have sprung from political bias against Trump. Amid such speculation, the *New York Times* ran a detailed description of the whistleblower without including the person's name.

During the now-famous phone call, Trump told Zelensky he wanted the Ukrainian government to investigate former vice president Joe Biden and his son Hunter (shown attending a college basketball game together in 2010).

The *Times* revealed that the whistleblower was a male Central Intelligence Agency (CIA) officer who worked at the White House. He had training as an analyst with special expertise on Ukrainian politics and policy. The *Times* also learned that the officer had not listened directly to Trump's July phone call. Instead, he had learned about the president's potential abuses from colleagues. They told him that future contacts between Trump and Zelensky rested on whether the Ukrainians would agree to investigate the Bidens. The whistleblower did not deliver the accusations to agency lawyers until one week after the call. The lawyers decided early on that his complaint had a reasonable basis and should go forward. From that point, news of the officer's concerns made its way through the CIA chain of command and on to the Justice Department and the White House. Concerned that the White House would bury the allegations, the officer decided to file an official whistleblower complaint with Atkinson.

The whistleblower's own lawyers refused to confirm the *Times* report. However, they did insist that publishing such information was dangerous. "Any decision to report any perceived identifying information of the whistle-blower is deeply concerning and reckless, as it can place the individual in harm's way," said Andrew Bakaj, the officer's lead counsel. "The whistle-blower has a right to anonymity."[7] Despite these warnings, details about the whistleblower continued to emerge. The *Washington Post* and the Associated Press added to the *Times*'s portrait of the CIA officer. Some conservative sites speculated about his identity and motives. In political circles, the officer's name was widely suspected. But although the media were under no obligation to keep the name secret, most outlets did. This held true for news media on both the political left and right.

> "Any decision to report any perceived identifying information of the whistle-blower is deeply concerning and reckless, as it can place the individual in harm's way."[7]
>
> —Andrew Bakaj, the attorney for the whistleblower

A Presidency in Constant Peril

The whistleblower's complaint and the resulting media frenzy returned Trump's presidency to a familiar place—seeming to teeter on disaster. Trump had already been subject to more scrutiny than any recent president. His status as a blustering outsider with no governing experience placed him at odds with official Washington from the start. His campaign pledge to "drain the swamp,"[8] or end what he claimed was the cronyism and corruption in Washington, may have thrilled his supporters, but it also enraged his opponents, who in turn accused Trump himself of engaging in nepotism and cronyism.

Among Capitol Hill insiders, predictions were rife that he would not serve out his term. Even on January 20, 2017, the day Trump had been sworn into office, a headline in the *Washington Post* had announced, "The Campaign to Impeach President Trump Has Begun." Lawrence Tribe, a Harvard law professor and one of the country's leading experts on constitutional law, thundered that

Trump "must be impeached for abusing his power and shredding the Constitution more monstrously than any other president in American history."[9] This remark came after Trump had been in office only two weeks.

The Trump White House had suffered from leaks that portrayed the president as out of his depth on foreign policy. Early in his administration, full transcripts of Trump's calls with the president of Mexico and the prime minister of Australia were leaked to the *Washington Post*, making it difficult going forward for him to hold high-level talks in private. Charges of conspiring with Russia sparked investigations by intelligence committees in both houses of Congress as well as by the Federal Bureau of Investigation (FBI), the CIA, and other intelligence agencies. FBI wiretaps of a Trump campaign official—later found to be based on questionable evidence—added to the scrutiny. Robert Mueller's special counsel investigation found insufficient evidence of a Trump-Russia conspiracy, but not before the president had faced nearly two years of further probes and dire predictions from the media. According to the *New York Times*, by September 2019, Trump was the subject of at least thirty investigations, including twelve congressional inquiries, ten criminal investigations at the federal level, and eight by state and local authorities. He had grown accustomed to daily chaos and accusations, with much of the turmoil caused by his own erratic behavior. In typical fashion, Trump continued to fire off combative tweets, rally his supporters, and chide his enemies for failing to bring him down.

The Trump-Zelensky Phone Call

The whistleblower complaint revived a concern from the first weeks of Trump's presidency. Worries about leaks had led the White House to clamp down on access to records of presidential phone calls. Nonetheless, on September 24, in an effort to defuse the crisis, the White House released a transcript-like summary of Trump's phone call with Ukraine's president. The document was not an exact re-creation of the call but was compiled

A Former CIA Official Raises Questions

The story of how the whistleblower's complaint reached Adam Schiff and the House Intelligence Committee does not lack for twists and turns. According to the *New York Times*, Schiff received a report about the complaint days before his committee got the actual complaint. In addition, the complaint showed evidence of having been carefully prepared by legal experts. Some Trump allies suspected the whistleblower himself was part of a larger effort to impeach the president.

In an opinion piece, Fred Fleitz, a former assistant to the National Security Council chief of staff, raised questions about the complaint after it was made public. "It appears to be written by a law professor," said Fleitz, "and includes legal references and detailed footnotes." Fleitz noted that in his experience, such written complaints are never so detailed and polished. He also pointed out that the complaint appeared shortly after Schiff had made numerous accusations about Trump withholding military aid to Ukraine. Fleitz pointed to a tweet of August 28, 2019, in which Schiff laid out a story almost identical to the whistleblower's complaint. Like others, Fleitz questioned why an allegation concerning Trump's phone call with a foreign leader would be considered an intelligence matter in the first place.

For Fleitz, it was vital that Republican lawmakers be able to cross examine the whistleblower about how he came to make his complaint. "I refuse to believe that the leaking, timing and presentation of this complaint is coincidence," said Fleitz. "I don't think the American people will buy this either."

Fred Fleitz, "Former CIA Official on Whistleblower: 'How Could This Be an Intelligence Matter?,'" *New York Post*, September 26, 2019. www.nypost.com.

from the notes of several officials who had listened in (as is common on such calls).

It revealed a relaxed exchange in which Trump first congratulated Zelensky on his April 2019 upset victory in Ukraine's presidential election. Then Trump made a pointed request: "I would like you to do us a favor though because our country has been through a lot and Ukraine knows a lot about it. I would like you to find out what happened with this whole situation with Ukraine. . . . I would like to have the Attorney General call you or your people and I would like you to get to the bottom of it."[10] The situation Trump referred to was the hacked computers of the Democratic National Committee. The president apparently believed discredited stories claiming the hacked server somehow wound up in Ukraine. No evidence exists for these claims.

Trump also wanted information about alleged Ukrainian aid to Hillary Clinton's 2016 campaign. After Zelensky agreed to help with these investigations, Trump referred to a Ukrainian prosecutor who was fired: "Good because I heard you had a prosecutor who was very good and he was shut down and that's really unfair. A lot of people are talking about that, the way they shut your very good prosecutor down and you had some very bad people involved."[11]

Trump was talking about Viktor Shokin, a Ukrainian official whose job included investigating the energy company Burisma Holdings. That is the company that Hunter Biden had joined as a board member in 2014. Shokin was fired in March 2016 for allegedly going easy on corrupt business figures. After encouraging Zelensky to call Rudy Giuliani, the president's personal lawyer and longtime friend, about Shokin, Trump focused on the Bidens: "The other thing, there's a lot of talk about Biden's son, that Biden stopped the prosecution and a lot of people want to find out about that so whatever you can do with the Attorney General would be great. Biden went around bragging that he stopped the prosecution so if you can look into it . . . it sounds horrible to me."[12]

> "The other thing, there's a lot of talk about Biden's son, that Biden stopped the prosecution. . . . So if you can look into it . . . it sounds horrible to me."[12]
>
> —President Trump

For Trump, the transcript-like summary was proof that the phone call contained nothing improper, that he had done nothing wrong. He claimed that he merely made a routine request for Zelensky's help in getting to the bottom of issues important to the United States. To others, however, the evidence of abuse of power was clear. Trump, they noted, had reminded Zelensky that the United States does a lot for Ukraine. With hundreds of millions of dollars in US military aid to Ukraine yet to be delivered, Trump had demanded an investigation of a political rival in exchange for the aid. This idea of a quid pro quo—giving something in order to get something—would become a key accusation in the impeachment inquiry.

Giuliani, Biden, and Corruption in Ukraine

According to Trump, one of his main goals in speaking to Zelensky was finding out whether the new Ukrainian president was committed to rooting out corruption in Ukraine. In June 2018, Trump had told a meeting of European leaders that Ukraine was one of the most corrupt countries in the world. Watchdog groups agreed. That same year, Transparency International ranked Ukraine as having high levels of corruption. Freedom House rated it second only to Russia in corruption among European nations. Frequent charges included bribery, kickbacks, and sweetheart deals for the oligarchs—or powerful business figures—who dominated Ukraine's economy. But Zelensky had campaigned on a promise of cleaning up his nation's corruption—and by most reliable accounts, he was trying to do just that. In addition to Trump's concern over Ukrainian corruption, he held a grudge related to the 2016 US election. In his view—which was widely disputed— Ukraine had taken steps to aid Clinton's campaign against him. This suspicion made him leery of dealing with Ukraine.

Trump enlisted Giuliani for the job of checking into Ukraine's anticorruption efforts. As a former prosecutor and one-time mayor of New York City, Giuliani had been through various political wars. And yet his role in the Ukrainian mess came under scrutiny. Critics questioned the propriety of a private citizen like Giuliani acting as the president's agent in a matter of foreign policy.

Some also pointed out that Giuliani had often spread conspiracy theories about the Bidens and alleged corruption in Ukraine. He clearly wanted Ukraine's investigators to pursue the Biden angle more vigorously. To Democrats and many in the media, Trump and Giuliani had little interest in Ukrainian corruption. Instead, they wanted to smear Joe Biden. As the whistleblower declared in his complaint, "The president's personal lawyer, Mr. Rudolph Giuliani, is a central figure in this effort."[13]

At the same time, Republicans noted that questions about the Bidens' dealings in Ukraine were not limited to conservative sources. In 2014 Hunter Biden was hired to serve on the board of Burisma Holdings, a Ukrainian oil and natural gas company. At the time, his father was overseeing policy on Ukraine for President Barack Obama's administration. This arrangement raised eyebrows in the State Department. Hunter had no experience in the energy field and never visited the country on company business during his tenure on the board. (Board meetings were held outside Ukraine.) Nonetheless, he was paid $50,000 a month, for a total of more than $3 million. During Hunter's time on the board, the Ukrainian government was investigating Burisma's owner for tax violations and money laundering. In December 2015, vice president Biden joined other Western nations in pressuring the Ukrainians to fire Shokin, the lead investigator. Reformers and Western diplomats considered Shokin to be corrupt and had been calling for his removal for months. The vice president threatened to withhold US loan guarantees if Shokin were not removed. Republicans likened this action to the actions of President Trump in his dealings with Ukraine.

The Trump-Ukraine controversy brought Hunter Biden into the media spotlight. During a September 2019 interview with ABC News, Biden said he only had one brief talk with his father about Ukraine. He recalled that his father told him, "I hope you know what you're doing."[14]

Raising More Questions

Despite the attention directed at the Bidens, it was the explosive whistleblower revelation that roiled Washington. Rather than easing pressure on the Trump White House, the release of the details of the conversation between Trump and Zelensky only raised more questions. On October 4, House Democrats began to issue subpoenas to White House officials, other administration figures, and Trump associates, including Giuliani. The impeachment inquiry was beginning to pick up speed.

Chapter Two

The House Impeachment Inquiry

When Gordon Sondland, the Trump administration's ambassador to the European Union, flew into Washington, DC, in early October 2019, he knew he was entering a hornet's nest of controversy. The former hotel magnate was scheduled to testify before Congress the next day about his role in the Ukraine scandal. According to reports at the time, Sondland had told Republican senator Ron Johnson of Wisconsin that President Trump's decision to delay nearly $400 million in military aid to Ukraine depended on the Ukrainians agreeing to investigate Biden and his son. Sondland denied the reports, saying Trump assured him there were no quid pro quos at all.

Sondland was ready to tell his story to Congress. However, on October 8, before the ambassador could testify, another bombshell erupted. The White House sent a letter to Congress announcing its refusal to cooperate with the House inquiry. Pat Cipollone, the president's attorney, protested that the closed-door hearings were unfair. He also contended that they were unconstitutional because the House had not voted to begin an official impeachment inquiry. Trump's defenders noted that the impeachment inquiries into Richard Nixon and Bill Clinton had both been authorized by a vote

22

of the full House. However, some experts defended Congress's approach, claiming that nothing in the Constitution or House rules requires a vote to start an impeachment inquiry. Trump responded by venting his anger via Twitter. "I would love to send Ambassador Sondland, a really good man and great American, to testify," Trump tweeted. "But unfortunately he would be testifying before a totally compromised kangaroo court"—meaning a court that ignores standards of justice—"where Republican's rights have been taken away, and true facts are not allowed out for the public to see."[15]

A White House Under Siege

The letter showed a White House under siege and lashing out in anger. Fresh difficulties seemed to arrive by the hour. Chairman Schiff of the House Intelligence Committee told reporters that failure to produce witnesses such as Sondland was strong evidence that Trump was obstructing Congress's investigation. In addition, a second

US Ambassador to the European Union Gordon Sondland is sworn in to testify before the House Intelligence Committee in November 2019. His testimony, originally scheduled for October, had been blocked by the White House.

whistleblower had come forward. Unlike the first one, this person claimed to have firsthand knowledge of the infamous phone call. The person did not file a separate formal complaint, but he or she received the same legal protections—including anonymity—while cooperating with the inspector general. It was unclear whether the second whistleblower had new information about the case. However, the second complaint served to support the idea that several government officials viewed Trump's phone call with alarm.

On October 4, House Democrats also released text messages dating from July to September 2019 between certain US diplomats, Giuliani, and Ukrainian officials. The messages contained discussions about how to pressure Zelensky into announcing an investigation into Trump's political rival. The diplomats, including Sondland and Kurt Volker, who was the special envoy to Ukraine, even drafted a statement for Zelensky to make and sent it to one of his aides. The aide wanted a guarantee of a White House visit for Zelensky—a major coup for a foreign leader—before he would agree to the statement. In the end, Zelensky never delivered the statement. But some of the messages seemed to affirm the quid pro quo arrangement. As William B. Taylor, the US ambassador to Ukraine, texted to Sondland, "Are we now saying that security assistance [military aid money] and WH [White House] meeting are conditioned on investigations?" Sondland, perhaps trying to avoid a written record of this idea, simply replied, "Call me."[16] Media reports suggested that the texts fleshed out the corrupt bargain that was implicit in Trump's phone call.

> "Are we now saying that security assistance [military aid money] and WH [White House] meeting are conditioned on investigations [in Ukraine]?"[16]
>
> —William B. Taylor, US ambassador to Ukraine

Despite the confusing swirl of Ukrainian names and diplomatic jargon, the American public was beginning to form opinions about the developing scandal. An NBC News/*Wall Street Journal* survey in early October found a 55 percent majority in favor of the impeachment inquiry. A Gallup poll done around the same time found that 52 percent of respondents thought Trump

Trump Versus Schiff

Throughout the Trump impeachment saga, Democratic lawmaker Adam Schiff played a leading role. As chair of the House Intelligence Committee, he was first to receive the whistleblower's complaint. He also presided over the first closed-door inquiries into Trump's alleged misconduct. After the House adopted articles of impeachment against the president, Schiff served as one of the House managers in the Senate trial. An October 4, 2019, *New York Times* editorial by legal expert Margaret L. Taylor was headed, "Adam Schiff Is the Right Man for the Moment."

Not surprisingly, Trump supporters had a different take. They recalled that during the Trump-Russia investigation (which Schiff led in the House), Schiff claimed to have direct proof that Trump conspired with the Russians. No such proof was ever produced. Some Republicans also voiced suspicions that Schiff and his staff coached the whistleblower on how to prepare his complaint to avoid legal hurdles. A spokesperson for Schiff denied the charge.

Schiff and Republican Devin Nunes, the ranking minority party member on the Intelligence Committee, have also had many conflicts. In an open letter, Nunes blasted Schiff for ignoring House rules. He noted that Schiff had sent records and other materials from the inquiry to the Judiciary Committee without first consulting him as ranking House member—which is required under House rules. Nunes wrote, "I urge you to put an immediate end to your vendetta against the President, stop your constant rule breaking, and begin treating this Committee and its oversight responsibilities with the seriousness they deserve."

Quoted in Brooke Singman, "Nunes Blasts Schiff for 'Blatant Disregard' of Impeachment Rules; Blames 'Vendetta' Against Trump," *Fox News*, December 8, 2019. www.foxnews.com.

should be impeached and removed from office, versus 46 percent who disagreed.

A Dispute over the Hearings

Of greater concern to the White House were the scheduled congressional hearings by the Intelligence, Oversight, and Foreign Affairs Committees, which were all controlled by Democrats. The committees—all of which included members from both parties—began to take depositions, or sworn testimony, from key figures in the Ukraine affair. The depositions were taken behind closed doors in a high-security room. Attendance at the hearings was strictly limited, with reporters and members of the public not allowed inside. Lawmakers who were not members of the committees also were barred from the proceedings. This push for secrecy drew strong protests from Republicans. They noted that the Nixon and Clinton impeachment hearings had been televised. They also complained about rules preventing Republican members from calling their own witnesses. Republicans and their conservative supporters believed the secret hearings were designed to produce a one-sided story.

However, Schiff and the Democrats defended the closed-door hearings as necessary to get at the truth. Schiff compared the hearings to a grand jury, which meets in secret to protect witnesses and prompt them to speak freely. He explained that the investigation into Trump's actions was just beginning, unlike past impeachment hearings in which most facts had already been established. Democrats also wanted to prevent witnesses from corroborating each other's stories. "Investigations are not public," declared Representative Ted Lieu, a Democrat from California. "When the investigation is done, there will be public hearings—that's how it's always been done."[17]

> "The letter [refusing to cooperate] is another avoidable self-inflicted wound by a White House that seems intent on counter-punching itself into an impeachment."[18]
>
> —Jonathan Turley, a constitutional law professor at George Washington University

Jonathan Turley, a constitutional law professor at the George Washington University, believed the White House was making a mistake by not cooperating with the inquiry. While he agreed that some of the Democrats' rules for the hearings were questionable, Turley noted that refusing to cooperate with a constitutional process could be considered an abuse of power. For Turley, "the letter [refusing to cooperate] is another avoidable self-inflicted wound by a White House that seems intent on counter-punching itself into an impeachment."[18]

Leaks and Angry Protests

The first round of hearings featured a parade of witnesses who would soon become public figures. Despite the White House vow not to cooperate, certain individuals, such as Marie Yovanovitch, the former US ambassador to Ukraine, did appear. Testimony during the closed-door hearings remained mostly secret. However, key parts were leaked to the media day by day. Nearly all of them were damaging to the president.

For example, one leak quoted Yovanovitch, whom Trump had fired in May 2019. She was allegedly let go after Trump learned that she was undermining his efforts to pressure Ukraine. She blamed her firing on Giuliani and other Trump cronies. "Although I understand that I served at the pleasure of the president," Yovanovitch told the committee, "I was nevertheless incredulous that

Former US Ambassador to Ukraine Marie Yovanovitch (pictured in 2018) testified despite the White House vow to not cooperate.

the U.S. government chose to remove an ambassador based, as best I can tell, on unfounded and false claims by people with clearly questionable motives."[19]

Other witnesses, such as Fiona Hill, formerly the administration's top adviser on Russia, described the deep concern about

The Question of Ukrainian Interference

One reason why President Trump remained wary of Ukraine was his belief that its government had worked against his campaign during the 2016 election. The media repeatedly claimed that this idea had long been debunked, or proved false. Fiona Hill and other National Security Council experts on Russia and Ukraine considered it a conspiracy theory.

These allegations first appeared on January 11, 2017, in a lengthy report by the left-leaning news magazine *Politico*. It published a long and detailed article about Ukraine's alleged interference. According to the article, Ukrainian government officials sought to undermine Trump's campaign by suggesting publicly he was unfit for office. Ukraine also accused Paul Manafort, a Trump associate who became his campaign manager, of corruption and announced intentions to investigate his consulting business. Manafort had been an adviser to disgraced former Ukrainian president and Russian ally Yanukovych. *Politico* discovered that Ukraine passed along other damaging accusations about Trump and his advisers to the Democratic National Committee. The report goes on to say, "*Politico*'s investigation found evidence of Ukrainian government involvement in the race that appears to strain diplomatic protocol dictating that governments refrain from engaging in one another's elections."

Politico and other media sources tried to minimize the importance of Ukrainian election interference when their earlier reports seemed to bolster Trump's claims about election meddling. As the right-leaning *Washington Examiner* put it in its own headline, "*Politico* Challenges *Politico*'s Reporting on Ukraine's 2016 Pro-Hillary Efforts."

Quoted in Kenneth P. Vogel and David Stern, "Ukrainian Efforts to Sabotage Trump Backfire," *Politico*, January 11, 2017. www.politico.com.

Becket Adams, "*Politico* Challenges *Politico*'s Reporting on Ukraine's 2016 Pro-Hillary Efforts," *Washington Examiner*, November 11, 2019. www.washingtonexaminer.com.

Trump's activities among senior foreign policy officials. Hill's leaked testimony revealed that national security adviser John Bolton had told her to tip off White House lawyers about possible illegal actions by the president. Another bombshell leak quoted Ambassador Taylor. He said that everything Zelensky wanted, including military aid and a White House visit, depended on his making a public vow to investigate the Bidens. Democrats argued that soliciting election help from a foreign government was an obvious abuse of power and could also be a violation of campaign finance laws.

With the leaked testimony leading the news each day, Republicans voiced their outrage at Schiff's secretive hearings. Trump's allies claimed that the public was not getting the straight story but was instead being fed targeted leaks. They objected that Republicans on the committee were not allowed to call witnesses. Republicans not on the committee complained that they were forbidden even to see transcripts of the testimony. (Noncommittee Democrats were not allowed access to the transcripts either.) On October 23, twenty-five Republican lawmakers barged into the committee room to protest Schiff's rules. Schiff quickly ended the session and threatened to sanction the violators. But Republicans continued to fume at the restrictions. As Representative Steve Scalise told reporters, "Voting members of Congress are being denied access from being able to see what's happening behind these closed doors, where they're trying to impeach the president of the United States with a one-sided set of rules."[20]

Public Hearings and the Human Element

The next stage of the impeachment process—the first public hearings—began on November 13. A House resolution passed in late October required Schiff to allow Republicans to suggest possible witnesses. However, their choices were still subject to approval by the committee's Democratic majority. In a public letter, ranking Republican member Devin Nunes of California blasted Schiff's tactics. Nunes said that traditional hearings allow for both sides to call witnesses without limits. He offered a list of ten potential witnesses whom he considered crucial. Among these were Hunter and Joe Biden. As Nunes argued, "[Hunter] Biden's firsthand experiences with Burisma can assist the American public in understanding the nature and extent of Ukraine's pervasive corruption, information that bears directly on President Trump's longstanding and deeply-held skepticism of the country."[21]

Nonetheless, Schiff and the Democrats held that the Bidens were not relevant to the investigation and made it plain they would not be called. As for Republican complaints about the inquiry process, Speaker Pelosi, Schiff, and other Democrats insisted that President Trump had forfeited many of his rights in the process by refusing to cooperate from the start. "If Donald Trump doesn't agree with what he's hearing, doesn't like what he's hearing, he shouldn't tweet. He should come to the committee and testify under oath," said Pelosi. "And he should allow all those around him to come to the committee and testify under oath."[22]

Before the public hearings began, the House released full transcripts of the closed-door testimony. Leaks from the private hearings somewhat blunted the impact of the release, as most of the key revelations were already known. However, interest quickly picked up on the third day of televised hearings, with the appearance of fired ambassador Yovanovitch. The impact of observing witness testimony, with all its tension and drama, riveted the attention of the American public.

Yovanovitch renewed her charge that Trump and Giuliani had conducted a smear campaign against her because she refused to go along with their pressure tactics against Ukraine. She told of her distress when she learned of Trump's barrage of criticism about her diplomatic career. She said that she felt threatened, and she saw no need for the president to smear her hard-earned reputation. Schiff suggested that Trump's Twitter attacks on Yovanovitch amounted to witness intimidation. Republicans were thus careful to praise her career during their questioning. Yovanovitch's testimony showed how the public's ability to see real witnesses via televised hearings might bolster the case against Trump.

Grilling a Star Witness

The second week of public hearings opened with the first witness to have actually listened in on Trump's July 25 call with Zelensky. Lieutenant Colonel Alexander Vindman, the top Ukraine specialist on the National Security Council (NSC), was considered to be a star witness for the Democrats. Early on, there was a sharp exchange between Vindman and Representative Nunes. When Nunes referred to the witness as "Mr. Vindman," the decorated officer, who appeared in full military regalia, insisted, "It's Lieutenant Colonel Vindman, please."[23] Vindman testified to the importance of Ukraine to US national security and said he was shocked to see how Trump was disrupting official policy toward Ukraine. With regard to the Biden controversy, Vindman declared, "It is improper for the president of the United States to demand a foreign government investigate a U.S. citizen and

Lieutenant Colonel Alexander Vindman, a top Ukraine specialist, testifies in November 2019. He described Ukraine as important to national security and expressed shock at Trump's actions toward Ukraine.

political opponent."[24] He stated that he considered it his duty to alert the top NSC lawyer about his concerns.

Concerned about the potential damage of Vindman's testimony, Republicans strained to undercut his statement. They asked him about an official memo in which Vindman's superior at the NSC had questioned his judgment. They noted that Vindman claimed not to know the name Burisma, despite his expertise on Ukraine. They hinted that Vindman had conspired with the whistleblower to bring down Trump. Some Republicans even questioned Vindman's loyalty to the United States—his family had fled Soviet-controlled Ukraine decades before—a tactic that outraged committee Democrats. Through his testimony, Vindman made clear his concern about the president's interaction with the Ukraine government, but he did not question the president's authority to determine US foreign policy. Asked whether Trump, in the phone call, had followed talking points based on official US policy toward Ukraine, Vindman said, "The president could choose to use the talking points or not. He's the president."[25]

In the afternoon session after Vindman's testimony, the committee heard from two witnesses who were expected to be helpful to Trump's case. Instead, they raised more questions about the president's behavior. Kurt Volker, the former special envoy to Ukraine, said Trump's focus on what Volker considered conspiracy theories about the 2016 election and Vice President Biden did nothing to support US security strategy with Ukraine. Timothy Morrison, the former senior director at the NSC, admitted his fears that Trump's phone call, if made public, would set off a political explosion.

Affirming a Quid Pro Quo

But the real surprise came during Ambassador Sondland's appearance on November 20. Sondland's story had undergone major changes. He had revised his first deposition, claiming his memory was refreshed after reviewing opening statements by

Taylor and former Trump adviser Morrison. Now Sondland said that numerous figures in the administration knew about the effort to pressure the Ukrainian president. Sondland declared that a White House meeting with Zelensky would only happen if Zelensky announced an investigation into Burisma and the Bidens. Sondland did not mince words: "Was there a 'quid pro quo?' As I testified previously, with regard to the requested White House call and White House meeting, the answer is yes."[26]

Another powerful witness against Trump appeared a day later. Like Volker, Fiona Hill testified that Trump's obsession with conspiracy theories about Ukraine and the Bidens undermined the NSC's policy of support for the new Ukrainian government. With impressive gravity, Hill observed that Trump, Giuliani, and aides like Sondland had tried to detour around NSC policy experts. "What I was angry with is: [Sondland] wasn't coordinating with us," she told the committee. "He was being involved in a domestic political errand [to get the Bidens], and we were being involved in national security, foreign policy, and those two things had just diverged." Hill added that she had warned Sondland, "'This is all going to blow up.' And here we are."[27]

A Scathing Report

Overall, the public hearings revealed a diplomatic corps mostly frustrated by Trump and skeptical of his aims. Two weeks after the hearings, Schiff and House Democrats released a three-hundred-page report on the investigation. The report found clear evidence that the president had solicited interference from Ukraine to help his reelection. It also accused Trump of obstructing the impeachment investigation. Republicans denounced the report. They claimed Trump was innocent of wrongdoing and was the victim of another political witch hunt. They noted that although the $391 million in military aid to Ukraine was delayed, it was eventually delivered without any public actions from Zelensky. The two sides remained deeply divided as the process edged toward a House vote on impeachment.

Chapter Three

The Impeachment Vote

The final step in the House inquiry was a look at the legal basis for impeaching President Trump. On December 4, 2019, the House Judiciary Committee heard from a panel of distinguished scholars in constitutional law. Three were invited by Democrats and one by Republicans. Their task was to review the history of impeachment in the United States, discuss the alleged behavior that had led to this inquiry, and offer their views on whether Trump's actions were impeachable. Those who watched the hearing got a crash course in American history, legal theory, and constitutional law. They heard discussions of what might be considered "high crimes and misdemeanors," the US Constitution's phrase for impeachable offenses. They also witnessed how political views can influence even the nation's top legal scholars. There was little debate or exchange of ideas. As political writer Russell Berman observed, "Democrats talked with the Democrats, Republicans talked with the Republicans, and the partisan lines that have been drawn on impeachment darkened a little bit more."[28]

"An Especially Serious Abuse of Power"

The law professors called by the Democrats—Noah Feldman of Harvard University, Michael Gerhardt of the University of North Carolina, and Pam Karlan of Stanford University—all agreed that Trump's conduct in the

Ukraine matter overwhelmingly called for impeachment. Feldman declared that the whole point of impeachment was to ensure that no president would be above the law. Gerhardt reckoned that Trump's misconduct included bribery and obstructing justice. He considered it far worse than the offenses that drove Richard Nixon from office. Karlan said that the essence of an impeachable offense is putting personal interest above national security concerns. She noted that the framers of the Constitution would have been horrified at Trump's seeking foreign influence on American elections. "That demand constituted an abuse of power," she told the committee. "Indeed, as I want to explain in my testimony, drawing a foreign government into our election process is an especially serious abuse of power because it undermines democracy itself."[29]

> "Indeed, as I want to explain in my testimony, drawing a foreign government into our election process is an especially serious abuse of power because it undermines democracy itself."[29]
>
> —Pam Karlan, a constitutional law professor at Stanford University

The Republicans' witness, Jonathan Turley of the George Washington University, held the opposite view from the other law professors, though with some reservations. He allowed that Trump's behavior could be impeachable, but he felt that the investigation had been rushed and left too many questions unanswered. "If the House proceeds solely on the Ukrainian allegations," said Turley, "this impeachment would stand out among modern impeachments as the shortest proceeding, with the thinnest evidentiary record, and the narrowest grounds ever used to impeach a president."[30]

The professors also addressed the view expressed by many Republicans that, with the 2020 election approaching, the decision on removing Trump should be left to voters. Feldman disagreed with this perspective. He stated that the framers of the Constitution feared a rogue president using his power to rig elections in his favor—and they adopted impeachment as the remedy for such abuses.

As for current American voters, the House hearings seemed to sway almost no one. A Reuters/Ipsos survey from early December 2019 found that opinions still broke along party lines. Seventy-eight

Four constitutional law experts—from left, Noah Feldman of Harvard Law School, Pamela Karlan of Stanford Law School, Michael Gerhardt of the University of North Carolina Law School, and Jonathan Turley of the George Washington University Law School—spoke to the constitutional grounds for impeachment.

percent of Democrats favored impeachment versus only 8 percent of Republicans. Overall, 44 percent of voters believed Trump should be impeached, and 42 percent were opposed.

Drafting the Articles of Impeachment

Immediately after the House hearings, Democrats moved forward with impeachment. Speaker Pelosi asked the main committee chairmen to draft articles of impeachment. This step almost ensured that the House would vote to impeach Trump by the end of the year. "His wrongdoing strikes at the very heart of our Constitution," Pelosi said in a brief televised address at the Capitol. "Our democracy is what is at stake."[31]

Some questioned why Pelosi and the Democrats were moving so swiftly. Trump had used claims of executive privilege—a doctrine that protects certain presidential communications from being revealed—to prevent a number of key witnesses from testifying. The courts had yet to rule on these claims. Testimony from witnesses close to Trump could possibly have strengthened the Democrats' case against the president. Nonetheless, Pelosi defended her strategy. She claimed that waiting for court decisions would only increase Trump's chances of soliciting more foreign interference in the upcoming election.

Ultimately, the House used the facts it had gathered to create two articles of impeachment. On December 10, House Judiciary chairman Jerrold Nadler of New York officially announced the filing of these articles. It was only the fourth time in US history that such articles had been drawn up against a sitting president. The first article accused Trump of abusing his power to further his own political ends. The second accused him of obstructing Congress in its investigation of the Ukraine matter. Members of the Judiciary Committee who drafted the articles said they wanted to focus on the most serious charges of misconduct. According to committee member David Cicilline of Rhode Island, "Abuse of power is the highest of high crimes and misdemeanors, and so that incorporates a lot of conduct."[32]

Still insisting that he had done nothing wrong, Trump dismissed the articles as flimsy and ridiculous. "There are no crimes," he told supporters at a campaign rally in Hershey, Pennsylvania. "They're impeaching me, and there are no crimes. This has to be a first in history."[33] Most Republicans backed the president, saying the articles were based on secondhand information and innuendo. Many conservative pundits noted that the charges were almost exactly the same as in the Mueller investigation—soliciting foreign election help and obstructing justice—as if Trump's enemies were determined to prove they were right all along. Democrats insisted, however, that the similarity showed a pattern of corrupt behavior by the president.

Before the articles were unveiled, a few Democrats from districts that Trump had won in 2016 floated an alternate plan. This plan was prompted by fears that impeachment would hurt their

At a December 2019 rally in Hershey, Pennsylvania, Trump insisted he had done nothing wrong and ridiculed the case for impeachment.

chances of reelection in those districts. They considered asking Republicans to join them in censuring the president for his behavior instead of impeaching him. A censure is an official reprimand, or rebuke, voted on by the entire House. The last-minute plan went nowhere.

An Emotional Debate

The stage was set for a fiery debate in the House Judiciary Committee. The two-day session was required to mark up the impeachment bill, or consider amendments to it before final passage. On the evening of December 11, the committee met to hear opening statements. Ordinarily, only the chair and the ranking minority member would deliver statements. However, owing to the historic circumstances, Chairman Nadler allowed all forty-one members to speak. A somber mood prevailed in the meeting room. Most of the members' statements laid out the same familiar arguments. The occasional partisan outburst was followed by a rustle of indignation by the opposite side. Chairman Nadler, in his remarks, challenged Republicans to think about how history would judge them. "You still have a choice. President Trump will not be president forever," he said. "When his time has passed, when his grip on our politics is gone, when our country returns—as surely it will—to calmer times and stronger leadership, history will look back on our actions here today. How would you be remembered?"[34]

The real fireworks began on the second day. Like a referee laying out the rules for a boxing match, Madeline Strasser, chief clerk for the judiciary panel, announced the resolution about the articles of impeachment. Partisan bickering erupted from the start. Members hurled personal insults without restraint. Chairman Nadler frequently had to pound the gavel to interrupt shouting matches. Members dredged up examples from past debates in order to accuse their opponents of hypocrisy. Republicans introduced a flurry of amendments to the proposed bill in a bid to dilute or eliminate the two articles of impeachment. These attempts led to hours of outraged speeches and angry accusations. Democrats accused Republicans of opting for partisanship over the good of the country. Republicans countered that the Democrats' impeachment effort was an attempt to overturn the 2016 election and showed nothing but contempt for the 63 million people who had voted for Trump.

> "When [Trump's] time has passed, when his grip on our politics is gone, when our country returns—as surely it will—to calmer times and stronger leadership, history will look back on our actions here today. How would you be remembered?"[34]
>
> —Jerrold Nadler, chairman of the House Judiciary Committee

As the session extended into the evening, the charges grew more heated. California Democrat Eric Swalwell blamed Trump for Ukrainian deaths due to his withholding of military aid. "People died in Ukraine at the hands of Russia," said Swalwell. "You may not want to think about that and it may be hard for you to think about that. But they died when this selfish, selfish president withheld the aid for his own personal gain."[35] Republicans dismissed Swalwell's accusation as ridiculous, noting that military funds were released well within the allotted time. Meanwhile, as the debate raged in the committee chamber, Trump dashed off a series of tweets about what he saw as a sham process. Brad Parscale, his campaign manager, told reporters that impeachment would only ignite more passionate support among the president's base.

With the session approaching its fourteenth hour, lawmakers on both sides consented to end the debate on amendments. The Republicans, being the minority party, were unable to pass a single proposal. California Republican Tom McClintock may have voiced the only remark with which all members could agree: "I have not heard a new point or an original thought from either side in the last three hours."[36] When Nadler postponed the final vote on the articles until the next morning, he angered his Republican colleagues. They accused him of seeking maximum publicity with a morning vote. On December 13, 2019, the bleary-eyed and still smoldering committee members gathered once more. Each article of impeachment was approved by a vote of 23 to 17, strictly along party lines.

> "It is tragic that the President's reckless actions make impeachment necessary. He gave us no choice."[37]
>
> —Nancy Pelosi, the Speaker of the House

The Vote to Impeach

The full House met on the following Wednesday to vote on impeachment. At this point, the outcome was never in doubt. As the majority party in the House, Democrats had a cushion of votes to ensure their desired result. Before the formal debate on the House floor, Speaker Pelosi delivered a brief preamble. "We gather today under the dome of this temple to exercise one of the most solemn powers that this body can take: The impeachment

Censuring the President

As the House moved toward a vote to impeach Donald Trump, some moderate Democrats suggested a milder form of rebuke. Their idea was to censure the president. If passed, censure would express the strong condemnation of the House regarding Trump's conduct in the Ukraine matter. Unlike impeachment, it would not lead to a Senate trial, and expulsion from office would not be an option. To some Democrats, it represented a practical compromise that even many Republicans might accept. For Democrats in otherwise pro-Trump districts, censure might be a way to save their jobs if Republican voters remained angry about impeachment in the fall. Moreover, the moderates noted, censure would enable Democrats to avoid a lengthy and contentious Senate trial, which might tilt public opinion toward the Republicans. In any case, because the ultimate decision would rest with the Senate (which had a Republican majority), removal from office was unlikely even if Trump were impeached.

Several House Republicans indicated that although they were unwilling to consider impeachment, they would possibly vote to censure Trump. However, most House Democrats gave the idea of censure little consideration. To them, Trump's behavior deserved nothing short of the ultimate rebuke. "If the goods are there, you must impeach," Pelosi told reporters. "Censure is nice, but it is not commensurate with the violations of the Constitution should we decide that's the way to go."

Quoted in Sarah Ferris and Melanie Zanona, "Small Group of Democrats Floats Censure Instead of Impeachment," *Politico*, December 10, 2019. www.politico.com.

of the President of the United States," said Pelosi. "If we do not act now we would be derelict [irresponsible] in our duty. It is tragic that the President's reckless actions make impeachment necessary. He gave us no choice."[37]

On December 18, 2019, eighty-five days after Pelosi had opened an investigation into the Ukrainian matter, President Trump was officially impeached. He became only the third president in history to be impeached. The final vote on the charge of abuse of power was 230 to 197. The vote on obstruction of justice was 229 to 198. Two moderate Democrats, from districts that had voted for Trump in 2016, cast votes against both articles. One Democrat voted in favor of only one article. Another Democrat voted "present" (meaning she took no position on either article). House Republicans unanimously opposed both impeachment articles.

After the vote, Pelosi sparked another controversy when she signed the bill. The Speaker wrote portions of her signature with various souvenir pens created for the signing ceremony. Each pen was handed out as a gift to a Democratic lawmaker. This kind of protocol is not unusual and is often reserved for special legislation. But Republicans felt that the souvenirs made a mockery of what should have been a solemn affair.

On December 18, 2019, House Speaker Nancy Pelosi presided over the votes to officially impeach President Donald Trump. He became only the third president in US history to be impeached.

Delaying Military Aid to Ukraine

Democrats like California's Eric Swalwell in the House impeachment inquiry made emotional claims that Trump's withholding of military aid to Ukraine cost soldiers' lives. Some media outlets picked up the theme, condemning Trump for leaving Ukrainian fighters helpless as they tried to fend off Russian aggression. But the *New York Times* reported that the main casualty from the freeze in spending was morale. "Ukrainian soldiers here at the front line were jolted by the suspension [of aid] too," wrote *Times* correspondent Andrew E. Cramer. "While the aid was restored in time to prevent any military setbacks, it took a heavy psychological toll, they said, striking at their confidence that their backers in Washington stood solidly behind their fight to keep Russia at bay."

According to a watchdog group in Ukraine, the United States provides 90 percent of the nation's military aid. As a result of this support, Ukraine's armed forces have undergone a vast improvement. Nonetheless, they still lack the naval and air power to defend against a full-scale Russian assault. President Zelensky and his top officials realize the importance of maintaining good relations with Washington, DC, in order to keep the funding pipeline open. They understand that a show of strength is necessary to deter Russian aggression. According to Cramer, even a temporary delay in US aid was worrisome for Ukraine. "It signaled their weakness," he says, "just as they were trying to project strength in negotiations with the Russians and needed solid backing from Washington."

Quoted in Andrew E. Cramer, "The Cost of Trump's Aid Freeze in the Trenches of Ukraine's War," *New York Times*, October 24, 2019. www.nytimes.com.

Weeks of Delay and Negotiation

The next step in the impeachment process required Speaker Pelosi to deliver the articles of impeachment to the Senate in preparation for a trial. Pelosi delayed this step for more than a month in hopes of negotiating more favorable rules for the Senate trial. Once the articles were delivered to the Senate, the balance of power would then shift to the Republicans. Senate majority leader

Mitch McConnell of Kentucky wielded enormous power over what went on in the upper chamber. McConnell and other Senate Republicans believed the impeachment was rushed, improper, and based on partisan rancor. They sought to end the matter with a swift trial. In fact, McConnell openly stated that he would work with White House lawyers in setting the ground rules for the trial.

During the delay, Pelosi pressured Senate Republicans to accept a key demand from Democrats: that the trial include witnesses. Since the impeachment vote, new evidence had emerged involving former national security adviser Bolton and others. Pelosi insisted that the country favored a full trial with witness testimony. "Over 70 percent of the American people think that the president should have those witnesses testify. So, again, it's about a fair trial," she told George Stephanopoulos of ABC News. "And we think that would be with witnesses and documentation. . . . Now the ball is in their court to either do that, or pay a price for not doing it."[38]

Meanwhile, McConnell had hinted that the Senate might vote to dismiss the whole matter if the articles were not delivered promptly. McConnell had plainly shown that he wanted a trial with no witnesses. However, he finally agreed that the question of witnesses could be considered after the trial's opening statements. Pelosi announced the House would soon be delivering the impeachment articles. After weeks of investigation and hearings in the House, the Senate trial of Donald Trump was about to begin.

Chapter Four

The Senate Trial

Shortly before the Senate trial began, a small group of moderate Republican senators held a private lunchtime meeting to discuss the rules of the trial. The senators included Alaska's Lisa Murkowski, Maine's Susan Collins, and Ohio's Rob Portman. Discussions among Republicans about how the trial might proceed had been going on since November, when it became obvious that Trump would be impeached. The key issue was witnesses. Allowing each side to call witnesses would certainly make for a more extended trial than Senate majority leader McConnell wanted. Yet some Republicans feared a backlash if they appeared to dismiss the charges against the president too hastily.

At the contentious lunch meeting, the moderate Republican senators discussed ways to signal that they were taking the impeachment trial seriously. Although they still rejected the idea of calling witnesses, they decided to ask McConnell to make other changes to his resolution on trial rules. One change provided both House impeachment managers and Trump's legal team three days instead of two for opening arguments. The second change allowed evidence from the House investigation to be admitted into the trial record automatically. These rule changes brought McConnell's trial plan into line with the process used in the Senate trial of President Clinton in 1999. Senate minority leader Chuck

Pictured in 2020, Lisa Murkowski of Alaska (left) and Susan Collins of Maine (right) were among a small group of moderate Republican senators who pushed for more time for opening arguments in the Senate trial.

Schumer saw the changes as proof that Republicans were feeling pressure to hold a genuine trial. "The public realizes how unfair the McConnell proposal is," Schumer told Capitol Hill reporters, "and the pressure that we have put on them and on Republican senators has gotten them to change. There are still many other things that are unfair, particularly in relationship to witnesses, particularly in relationship to documents."[39] Clashes over fairness would continue throughout the proceedings.

A Battle over the Rules of Evidence

The impeachment trial of President Trump began on January 16, 2020. The first day featured ceremonial functions, including a reading of the House articles of impeachment. The important business got under way five days later. Under the Constitution, the chief justice of the United States presides over the trial. In this case, that duty fell to Chief Justice John Roberts. The seven managers for the House case—in effect, the prosecutors—included lead manager Schiff, chair of the House Intelligence Committee; Judiciary chairman Nadler; and Representative Zoe Lofgren of California. Trump's defense team featured, among others, White House counsel Pat Cipollone, Trump's personal attorney Jay Sekulow, Harvard Law School professor Alan Dershowitz, and former special prosecutor Kenneth Starr. Sworn to silence and forbidden even to use cell phones, senators sat at their desks, arrayed around the central marble podium and Chief Justice Roberts. The Senate consisted of fifty-three Republicans, forty-five Democrats, and two independents who tended to vote with the Democrats.

A battle broke out immediately over the rules of evidence. House managers pressed for the right to subpoena key witnesses and documents. They wanted testimony from White House officials plus documents that were being withheld. During twelve hours of debate, they argued that these steps were crucial to show the true dimensions of Trump's abuse of power. "With the backing of a subpoena authorized by the chief justice of the United States, you can end President Trump's obstruction," said Lofgren, who was the first woman to address the Senate as an impeachment manager. "If the Senate fails to take this step, you won't even ask for the evidence. This trial and your verdict will be questioned."[40]

Nonetheless, in a series of party-line votes, Republicans rejected each attempt to change the rules. Nadler accused Republican senators of a cover-up, which drew angry rebuttals from Trump's lawyers. They asked why Democrats needed more evidence if they

> "It's long past time that we start this, so we can put an end to this ridiculous charade and go have an election."[41]
>
> —Pat Cipollone, the White House counsel

thought Trump's guilt had already been proved. Moreover, the Trump team continued to say that the impeachment was a partisan stunt. "It's long past time that we start this," Cipollone, the White House counsel, told senators, "so we can put an end to this ridiculous charade and go have an election."[41] Just before 1 a.m., the wrangle between the House managers and Trump's legal team became so raucous that Roberts had to urge both sides to remember where they were and engage in civil discourse.

House Managers Make Their Case

On January 22, House managers began their case by setting out a timeline of events. According to the rules adopted, they had twenty-four hours over three days to present their case. Schiff and the other managers walked through the story revealed by the six-week House probe. They first described an April 21, 2019, phone call in which Trump invited Zelensky for a White House meeting. They reviewed Trump's July phone call, and his request for an investigation of Biden and his son. They laid out the alleged quid pro quo of releasing nearly $400 million in military aid to Ukraine and hosting Zelensky at the White House only in exchange for the announcement of an investigation of the Bidens. They noted the behind-the-scenes maneuvering by the president's aides and outside associates such as Rudy Giuliani. These efforts, they argued, sought to pressure Zelensky to investigate the Bidens and Burisma. In the end, said the House managers, Trump tried to cheat, got caught, then tried to cover up his misconduct. The managers' chronological presentation also included video clips of key testimony from the House hearings, especially from the NSC experts on Ukraine. As Schiff summed up the case, "[Trump] does not under our laws and under our Constitution have a right to use the powers of his office to corruptly solicit foreign aid—prohibited foreign aid—in his reelection. . . . And he certainly does not have the right to undermine our elections and place our security at risk for his own personal benefit."[42]

The next day saw the House managers lay out the case for the charge of obstruction of Congress. Representative Val Demings of Florida provided several examples of Trump directing officials in the executive branch not to testify or not to give up documents the House had subpoenaed. Demings claimed this was a misuse of presidential power. She also renewed the argument for calling new

Trump's Claim of Executive Privilege

President Trump and his team of lawyers threatened to invoke executive privilege if senators tried to subpoena witnesses or documents in his impeachment trial. Executive privilege is a president's formal right to shield certain private communications in the public interest. It is intended to ensure that presidents can speak freely with advisers and other members of the executive branch without fear of public disclosure. Trump said his claim of executive privilege would not only protect his own administration but also those in the future. Observers noted that his claim would likely be challenged all the way to the Supreme Court. In this way, Trump could prolong the outcome of his Senate trial for months.

Nonetheless, many legal experts questioned whether Trump's claim of executive privilege would hold up in court. Historians pointed out that several presidents, including George Washington, had assumed that an impeachment inquiry would override claims of executive privilege. This would prevent lawless presidents from hiding their misconduct. As President James K. Polk wrote in 1846, "In [an impeachment] case the safety of the Republic would be the supreme law, and the power of the House in the pursuit of this object would penetrate into the most secret recesses of the Executive Department." In 1974 that idea was upheld in President Nixon's case. The Supreme Court ruled that Nixon could not claim executive privilege to shield secret incriminating tapes from a congressional inquiry. This ruling led to Nixon's resignation.

Quoted in Garrett Epps, "Congress Should Go to the Supreme Court Right Away," *The Atlantic*, October 1, 2019. www.theatlantic.com.

witnesses and examining all documents. "Over time these documents and this evidence will undoubtedly come to light and I ask this body to not wait to read about it in the press or in a book," said Demings. "You should be hearing this evidence now."[43]

In an hour-long history lesson on impeachable conduct, Nadler asserted that finding an actual crime is not necessary for impeachment. He quoted past statements from South Carolina senator

Lindsey Graham, Attorney General William Barr, and Trump attorney Dershowitz in which they indicated their belief that abuse of power was sufficient grounds to remove a president. House managers also offered a lengthy defense of Hunter Biden. They declared there was no evidence that Hunter had done anything illegal, and they said his work for Burisma was not relevant to the charges against Trump. Vice President Joe Biden's push to get a corrupt Ukrainian prosecutor fired was, they claimed, perfectly valid as part of the Obama administration's efforts to fight corruption in Ukraine.

Schiff and the House managers wrapped up their arguments on January 24. They stressed that additional witnesses and papers would add a wealth of detail to their case against Trump. An ABC News/*Washington Post* poll found that two-thirds of Americans agreed that the Senate should call witnesses. Meanwhile, behind closed doors, Republicans once more discussed the idea of calling witnesses and nixed it again. The fear was that Trump would claim executive privilege. The resulting court challenges could last for months and tie up Senate business all the way to the November election.

House managers, led by Representative Adam Schiff of California (center), speak to the media about the Senate impeachment trial. At the start of the trial, they established a timeline of events.

The President's Defense Begins

The first day of President Trump's defense fell on Saturday, January 25, 2019. This led his legal team to protest that no one would be watching. Trump, the former reality television star, agreed about the timing on Twitter. "Looks like my lawyers will be forced to start on Saturday," he tweeted, "which is called Death Valley in T.V."[44]

In a brief two-hour session, Trump's team got off to what legal experts considered a rocky start. They again attacked the Democrats' impeachment push as motivated by politics. They claimed the president had good reasons to withhold military aid from Ukraine, and they said the hold was only temporary. They also argued that the House managers had ignored facts in Trump's favor while presenting a one-sided case. For example, Trump's lawyers noted that when questions arose about the July phone call with Zelensky, Trump released a rough transcript, compiled from officials' notes, of the entire call. White House counsel Cipollone said the president deserved credit for his transparency in the matter.

> "If there's any unfairness in these proceedings, it's the astounding mismatch between the high skill and preparation of the House managers and the rambling, dissembling and gaslighting of [Trump's] counsel. It's like the New York Yankees versus the Bad News Bears."[45]
>
> —George Conway, a conservative lawyer and Trump critic

However, even some conservatives felt that Trump's legal team seemed to be flailing, with no overall strategy. Instead of answering the Democrats' charges, Trump's lawyers continued to complain about issues of fairness. This tactic had brought scorn from Trump opponents since the trial's first day. "If there's any unfairness in these proceedings, it's the astounding mismatch between the high skill and preparation of the House managers and the rambling, dissembling and gaslighting of [Trump's] counsel," tweeted George Conway, a conservative lawyer and Trump critic. "It's like the New York Yankees versus the Bad News Bears."[45]

Meanwhile, another bombshell leak led to renewed calls among Democrats for witnesses. The *New York Times* reported on a not-yet-published book by former national security adviser

Bolton. A description of portions of the manuscript was leaked to the *Times*. The newspaper reported that in the manuscript Bolton claimed Trump told him he wanted to hold back aid to Ukraine until it agreed to investigate the Bidens. Many believed Bolton's story could show Trump's true intent. Senate Democrats joined House managers in pushing for Bolton to testify. Some Republican senators, like Utah's Mitt Romney, were willing to entertain the idea of calling Bolton and other witnesses. As Romney noted, "It's pretty fair to say that John Bolton has a relevant testimony to provide to those of us who are sitting in impartial justice."[46]

Focusing on Ukraine and Corruption

The next day Attorney Sekulow sidestepped the Bolton news that had gripped the capital. Instead, Trump's team turned to the issue of Ukrainian corruption. They insisted that with Ukraine's recent history of corrupt practices, Trump had every reason to

In a not-yet-published book, former national security adviser John Bolton (pictured) reportedly claimed that Trump told him to hold back aid to Ukraine until it agreed to investigate the Bidens.

John Bolton's Bombshell Book

The word *bombshell* exploded across the media landscape on January 27, 2020. Amid the Senate impeachment trial, the *New York Times* reported that a book by former national security adviser John Bolton was about to be published. According to information obtained by the *Times*, in the book Bolton would describe Trump telling him that military aid to Ukraine would not be released unless and until the Ukrainian president agreed to an investigation of presidential candidate Joe Biden. If true, Bolton's claim was proof of the so-called quid pro quo arrangement for which Trump was on trial. The leak seemed sure to spawn renewed calls among Democrats for witnesses, including Bolton.

After the *Times* report, Bolton himself came under fire from former allies. The fiery, hawkish Bolton had always enjoyed the favor of staunch conservatives. Now, however, he faced accusations that he was betraying Trump. Some conservatives painted Bolton as disgruntled and out for revenge after Trump fired him. In any case, Republican senators felt new pressure to allow witnesses. Media pundits debated whether Republicans would resist the pressure. "There's a very real possibility that Republican senators, prioritizing Trump's needs over the rule of law and the search for truth, will continue to resist calling Bolton to testify," said MSNBC's Steve Benen. "This would make a mockery of the process, and turn the impeachment trial into a punch-line for a sad joke, but it may happen anyway."

Steve Benen, "Why Bolton's Book Bombshell Has Jolted the Impeachment Debate," MSNBC, January 27, 2020. www.msnbc.com.

be wary. Moreover, they said Trump had already been the victim of Ukrainian double-dealing. They referred to detailed reports on how Ukraine had worked behind the scenes to aid the Clinton campaign in 2016. (Most mainstream media and US intelligence sources contended these reports had been debunked.)

Trump's legal team also claimed that Zelensky never knew that military aid was being withheld. Thus, in their view, he could not have felt pressured to do anything. And, in the end, he never opened an investigation of the Bidens. Trump's team also examined Hunter Biden's affiliation with the Ukraine energy company Burisma. Attorney Eric Herschmann, former assistant district attorney in Manhattan, New York, suggested that Hunter's placement on Burisma's board looked corrupt on its face. It was natural, he said, for Trump to be concerned. Herschmann questioned why the younger Biden was paid such a huge sum despite his lack of experience in the energy field.

"Why do they want to pay him millions of dollars?" Herschmann asked. "Well, he did have one qualification, he was a son of the vice president of the United States. He was the son of the man in charge of the Ukrainian portfolio for the prior administration and we are to believe there is nothing to see here, that for anyone to investigate or inquire about this would be a sham."[47]

After the session, there was talk that Trump's lawyers had found their footing. Republican senators praised their performance. They thought the legal team had rebutted the House managers' defense of the Bidens with pertinent information. Probably no minds were changed on either side, but Trump's team had at least made a substantial case for his acquittal.

Holding Out Hope for Bolton

Democrats still held out hope that McConnell and the Republicans could be pressured into calling witnesses, enabling America to hear Bolton's potentially explosive testimony. For Democrats, Bolton was the "smoking gun" witness capable of proving Trump's corrupt intent. "If you have any question about [Trump's actions] at all, you need to hear from his former national security adviser. Don't wait for the book," said Schiff. "We think the case is overwhelmingly clear without John Bolton, but if you have any question about it, you can erase all doubt."[48] Settlement of the witness question would be the last major hurdle for both sides in the Trump impeachment drama.

Chapter Five

Verdict and Aftermath

During most of the impeachment trial, senators had been required to sit and listen silently. For two days, beginning on January 29, 2020, they finally got the opportunity to ask questions. Alternating by party, senators submitted written questions to Chief Justice Roberts. After reading each question aloud, Roberts allowed the House managers and Trump's legal team to respond. On the first day, most of the questions were friendly prompts to go over key points in the proceedings. Democrats tossed their softballs to the House managers, Republicans to the Trump lawyers. One interesting reaction arose over a question from Republican senator Rand Paul of Kentucky. Roberts glanced at the question, then announced, "The presiding officer declines to read the question as submitted."[49] He considered it an attempt by Paul to reveal the name of the whistleblower. The incident caused some conservative opinion writers to revive their argument that the whistleblower's identity—and motives—were relevant to Trump's impeachment.

Avoiding Some Controversies, Courting Others

After the session, Paul shared his question with the media. In it, he named both a staff member for Schiff's House Intelligence Committee and the alleged whistleblower.

His question asked if House managers knew whether the staff member and alleged whistleblower had worked together to plot impeachment before the formal House proceedings. Roberts's refusal to read the question aloud showed that many in Washington—foremost among them the chief justice of the United States—were dedicated to upholding the protections granted to whistleblowers. With tensions in the chamber running high, many Republican senators, including Lindsey Graham and Senate majority leader McConnell, agreed that Roberts did the right thing in not sparking a new controversy.

Media outlets kept close watch on questions from moderate Republicans, including Senators Susan Collins, Mitt Romney, Lisa Murkowski, and Lamar Alexander. These were the senators whom Democrats hoped to sway in the final vote on calling witnesses. At one point, Collins asked why the House managers had not charged Trump with bribery since they insisted there was overwhelming proof he was guilty of that offense. The managers

Chief Justice John Roberts reads a question during the question-and-answer portion of the Trump impeachment trial. Roberts rejected one questioner's attempt to reveal the whistleblower's identity.

had argued that Trump's quid pro quo deal with Zelensky was basically a bribe. "We could have charged bribery," Schiff said in response. "In fact, we outlined the facts that constitute bribery in the article, but abuse of power is the highest crime. . . . The facts we allege within that do constitute bribery."[50] Observers wondered whether Collins's question was a hint that her mind was not made up about the case. Perhaps she and the other moderates might be open to calling additional witnesses.

The Vote on Witnesses

The question of witnesses, having hung over the impeachment trial from the first day, finally came to a vote on January 31. For weeks, both sides had floated names of people they would like to hear from. Democrats focused on former national security adviser Bolton and Lev Parnas, a Russian-born businessman who had worked with Giuliani on Ukraine. Republicans suggested that they might subpoena Hunter Biden, but mainly they stressed that Democrats should have dealt with the witness question in the House inquiry. In reality, most Republican senators wanted nothing to do with witnesses. They sought to get the trial over with as quickly as possible. As for Democrats, they hoped that a successful vote for witnesses would further strengthen their case against the president.

Ultimately, the Senate voted 51 to 49 not to subpoena witnesses. Two Republicans—Mitt Romney and Susan Collins— broke ranks and voted with the Democrats, but it was not enough. Afterward, some Republicans agreed that the evidence showed Trump was guilty of misconduct in his dealings with Ukraine. But they believed it was not sufficient grounds for removing a duly elected president. "It was inappropriate for the president to ask a foreign leader to investigate his political opponent and to withhold United States aid to encourage that investigation," said Senator Alexander of Tennessee. "But the Constitution does not give the Senate the power to remove the president from office and ban him from this year's ballot simply for actions that are inappropriate."[51]

The vote effectively brought Trump's impeachment trial to a close. Some in the media noted that the final vote on whether or not to convict the president of the two charges would not take place until after his State of the Union speech. Thus, Trump would be unable to use the speech to declare victory. But Democrats remained frustrated. It had been the shortest impeachment trial in history, and the only one without witnesses. "[Trump] cannot claim a true acquittal if this has not been a fair trial," said California senator Kamala Harris. "In every impeachment hearing, be it for a judge or a president, that has gone through completion, witnesses have been presented at the trial."[52]

Voting on a Verdict

Another day was taken up with closing arguments, which, in this case, was a largely ceremonial requirement. Arguments for both sides had been repeated so often that they fell flat. The Monday session found senators distracted by other news. The Iowa caucuses, a crucial step in the nominating process for president, were scheduled for the next day, as was the State of the Union address. After weeks of pitched battles in the House and Senate, many legislators just wanted a rest. The public remained split on the issue of removing the president from office. A *Politico*/Morning Consult poll on February 1 showed 50 percent approval for convicting Trump and 43 percent opposed. Nonetheless, television ratings for the Senate trial indicated only mild interest in the proceedings.

Results of the Iowa caucuses emerged on February 4, 2020, the day after the voting. Former vice president Biden finished fourth. He admitted the disappointing result was a "gut punch."[53] Experts disagreed on whether discussions in the trial about Biden, his son, Burisma, and Ukrainian prosecutors had damaged the Biden campaign in Iowa.

Later that night, Trump delivered a rambling State of the Union speech that was well received by his Republican supporters but panned by Democrats. The president neglected the traditional handshake with Speaker Pelosi prior to the speech. During the

Romney's Vote to Convict

One Republican who received a measure of praise from political commentators was Utah senator Mitt Romney. By voting yes on the abuse of power charge against Trump, Romney became the only Republican senator to endorse convicting the president. Many reporters marveled that Romney, a Republican heavyweight who had been his party's unsuccessful candidate for president in 2012, should cross party lines on such a high-profile vote. Chairman Schiff also expressed appreciation. "I have great respect for the moral courage that he showed," Schiff said. "He showed you can stand up to this president. And you can put truth and decency first."

The president, however, had only disparaging remarks for Romney. "Mitt Romney is forever bitter that he will never be POTUS," Trump tweeted. "He was too weak to beat the Democrats then so he's joining them now." Romney, in Trump's view, represented the Republican establishment that Trump had been railing against for years. Trump was sure to remember what he considered to be Romney's betrayal. In April 2020, when Trump was gathering Republican senators for a meeting on the coronavirus issue, Romney was the only one not invited to take part.

Associated Press, "Mitt Romney Draws Praise, Condemnation as Sole Republican Voting to Convict Trump," February 5, 2020. www.marketwatch.com.

evening, he made no mention of impeachment. When Trump finished his address, Pelosi pointedly ripped her copy of his speech in two in full view of the television cameras.

The next day, on February 5, the full Senate gathered once more for the final vote. The outcome was much less in question than the vote on witnesses had been. Sixty-seven votes were required to convict the president and remove him from office, meaning Republicans needed only thirty-four votes to acquit Trump. The final tally on both articles of impeachment was nearly a straight party-line vote. Senators rejected the first article, abuse of power, by a total of 52 to 48. The second, obstruction of Congress, was rejected by a count of 53 to 47. Romney broke with his party to vote yes on removing Trump for obstruction. He was the only Republican to do so.

Emotional Reactions

Even with the trial's outcome a foregone conclusion, emotions ran high in response to the Senate's verdict. Trump tweeted that he had done nothing wrong and railed against the so-called deep state that had failed once more to take him down. He bashed Romney for defecting from his party and voting to convict Trump in the Senate. He also taunted his Democratic foes with a tweeted video showing him successfully running for president again and again, suggesting he would be president "4EVA."[54] His supporters among the public expressed joy and relief at the acquittal. Some hoped that Congress would put aside their differences with the president and get back to work. "They're going to have to re-

On February 5, 2020, the Senate rejected both articles of impeachment. The vote totals on the second article of impeachment—obstruction of Congress—are shown in the Senate chambers shortly after the vote.

GUILTY 47 NOT GUILTY 53

The question is on

Article Two

ally stand up and focus on the people instead of on the negativity of Trump," said Patricia Studie, a beautician in Loveland, Colorado. "You know, people get sick and tired of hearing about it. We want to hear, what are they going to do for this country?"[55]

Yet columnists across the nation countered that the impeachment trial *was* Congress doing its job, and they blasted Republican senators for bailing out a president widely seen as reckless and corrupt. "Republicans who have chosen party and despot over country and law must be made to pay at the ballot box in November," wrote Charles M. Blow in the *New York Times*. "If a majority of the Senate cannot be expected or made to do the right thing, the Senate majority must be changed. It must be defeated."[56]

Other writers, while dismayed at Trump and the Republicans, also blamed Democrats for a flawed and futile impeachment effort. Many faulted Pelosi for rushing through the impeachment and then delaying the trial for a month for what they considered no good reason. For many young people, the whole affair was disheartening. "I feel almost betrayed," said Gabriel Enrikes, a sophomore at West Los Angeles College. "I feel like everything that I've learned as a political science major and a U.S. citizen has been a lie because I do feel that President Trump did something wrong, and I feel like he went unpunished. So it's made me really question how seriously we actually take the Constitution and the office of the president."[57] Across the country, nearly everyone forecast even more dismal relations between the parties in Congress through the November elections.

> "I feel almost betrayed. I feel like everything that I've learned as a political science major and a U.S. citizen has been a lie because I do feel that President Trump did something wrong, and I feel like he went unpunished."[57]
>
> —Gabriel Enrikes, a sophomore at West Los Angeles College

Payback and Outrage

Trump's critics also predicted he would take the first opportunity to pay back those who had testified against him. It did not take long for those fears to come true. Just two days after his acquittal, the president and the White House took action against two key witnesses in the House inquiry. First, Trump fired Lieutenant Colonel Vindman, the national security aide and top expert on Ukraine. Vindman had been a key witness against Trump in the House impeachment inquiry. Vindman and his twin brother, Yevgeny, were both escorted out of the White House by Secret Service personnel. Vindman's lawyer, David Pressman, left no doubt that he believed his client's ouster was political payback. "There is no question in

Praise and Blame for a Fired Watchdog

For Democrats, former inspector general Michael Atkinson remains one of the true heroes of the Trump impeachment story. As an intelligence community watchdog, Atkinson ensured that the whistleblower's complaint was delivered to Congress. He did not allow the skepticism of DNI Joseph McGuire to sway his decision. When Trump gave Atkinson his notice, ending his tenure as inspector general, many commentators were outraged. To them, it was an example of cheap payback against a person who showed great integrity, a slap that Atkinson certainly did not deserve.

Trump supporters, however, saw Atkinson's role in a less positive light. They claimed that Atkinson had ignored some of the statutory requirements for whistleblowers in the intelligence community. For example, for a complaint to be valid, it must relate "to the funding, administration, or operation of an intelligence activity" under the authority of the DNI. But the whistleblower's complaint concerned the commander in chief, who governs the intelligence community but is not part of it. Atkinson's office also changed the official whistleblower form to remove the requirement for firsthand information. The whistleblower got his version of the phone call, from a colleague who had been asked to listen in. With these and other irregularities in mind, Attorney General William Barr and other Justice Department officials believed Trump had reasonable cause to fire Atkinson.

Office of the Inspector General of the Intelligence Community, "Disclosure of Urgent Concern Form—Unclassified." www.dni.gov.

the mind of any American why this man's job is over, why this country now has one less soldier serving it at the White House," Pressman told reporters. "The truth has cost LTC Alexander Vindman his job, his career, and his privacy."[58]

Later that same day, Ambassador Sondland was recalled from his post in Brussels. Sondland had testified to learning about Trump's push for a quid pro quo deal with Ukraine. After he was informed of his dismissal, Sondland offered no protest and said he was grateful for the opportunity to serve.

On April 3, Trump provoked more outrage from critics by giving notice of termination to Inspector General Atkinson, the intelligence community watchdog who had passed along the whistleblower's complaint to Schiff and the House Intelligence Committee. Democrats blasted the president for what they saw as a campaign of revenge. Schiff called it "another blatant attempt by the President to gut the independence of the Intelligence Community and retaliate against those who dare to expose presidential wrongdoing."[59]

Editorial pages crackled with anger at the firings. Many pundits feared that Trump, having escaped removal in his Senate trial, would now feel free to engage in even more dangerous behavior than before. In the *Washington Post*, the whistleblower's lawyers raised alarms about Trump's retaliation against the watchdogs. "President Trump's purge of our nation's inspectors general is a crisis," wrote the team led by Andrew Bakaj. "It is a crisis that has a direct impact on the health and safety of all Americans, as well as the democratic protections that keep us from slipping into corruption. Alarm bells should be going off everywhere."[60]

From One Crisis to a Larger Crisis

Meanwhile, as headlines focused on impeachment, alarms were sounding about another crisis. Trump and his inner circle had no

> "There is no question in the mind of any American why this man's job is over, why this country now has one less soldier serving it at the White House. The truth has cost LTC Alexander Vindman his job, his career, and his privacy."[58]
>
> —David Pressman, a lawyer for Lieutenant Colonel Vindman

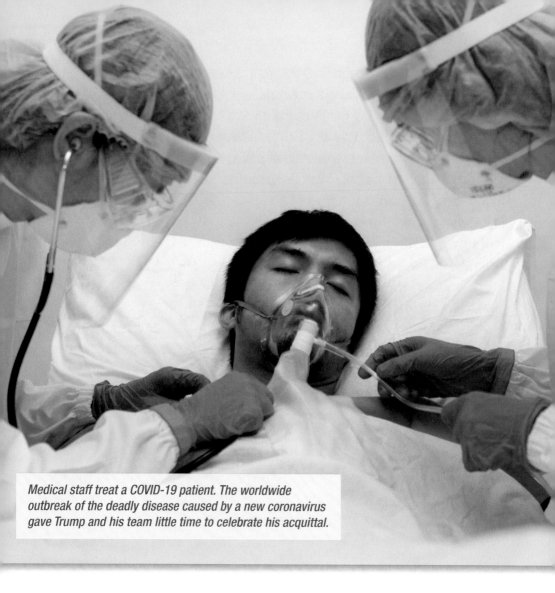

Medical staff treat a COVID-19 patient. The worldwide outbreak of the deadly disease caused by a new coronavirus gave Trump and his team little time to celebrate his acquittal.

time to celebrate his acquittal. The worldwide outbreak of a deadly coronavirus threatened to upend daily life in the United States. On January 31, with his impeachment trial winding down, Trump restricted most travelers from China, where the viral outbreak began, from entering the United States. Over the next few weeks, the Trump administration focused its attention on dealing with the outbreak. For lawmakers, after months of wrangling and bitter recriminations over impeachment, it was imperative that they work together and with the Trump administration to address the mounting health crisis.

Some in Congress also discussed making changes to the impeachment process. Not surprisingly, the proposed changes often split along party lines. Florida Republican senator Rick Scott proposed a constitutional amendment raising the voting requirement for passing articles of impeachment to three-fifths of the House, instead of a simple majority. Oregon Democratic senator Jeff Merkley suggested a Senate rule guaranteeing that new witnesses and documents be admitted for all future impeachment trials. However, several lawmakers recommended postponing consideration of such changes. As Missouri Republican senator Roy Blunt advised, "We have to give it a pretty significant cooling-off period before getting back into how these rules should work."[61] After a bruising impeachment fight involving one of the most polarizing presidents ever, that seemed to be the consensus among lawmakers and the public.

Source Notes

Introduction: A Phone Call Sets Off a Firestorm

1. Quoted in Kate Brannen, "Trump's True Betrayal: A Pattern of Soliciting Foreign Interference in US Elections," Just Security, December 3, 2019. www.justsecurity.org.
2. Quoted in Karoun Demirjian, Mike DeBonis, and Matt Zapotosky, "Trump Said His Ukraine Call Was 'Perfect.' Impeachment Witnesses Testified Otherwise," *Washington Post*, November 19, 2019. www.washingtonpost.com.

Chapter One: The Whistleblower's Complaint

3. Quoted in Zachary Cohen, "Whistleblower Controversy Thrusts Little-Known Trump Appointee into the Limelight," CNN, September 30, 2019. www.cnn.com.
4. Quoted in Cohen, "Whistleblower Controversy Thrusts Little-Known Trump Appointee into the Limelight."
5. Quoted in Brett Samuels, "Trump Decries Whistleblower Story as 'Another Media Disaster,'" *The Hill*, September 20, 2019. www.thehill.com.
6. Quoted in John Parkinson, "6 Key Takeaways from Top Intel Official's Testimony on Whistleblower Complaint," ABC News, September 26, 2019. www.abcnews.go.com.
7. Quoted in Julian E. Barnes et al., "White House Knew of Whistle-Blower's Allegations Soon After Trump's Call with Ukraine Leader," *New York Times*, September 26, 2019. www.nytimes.com.
8. Quoted in Peter Overby, "Trump's Efforts to 'Drain the Swamp' Lagging Behind His Campaign Rhetoric," National Public Radio, April 26, 2017. www.npr.org.

9. Quoted in Gene Healy, "Lawrence Tribe's Impeachment Hysteria," *National Review*, June 23, 2017. www.nationalreview .com.

10. Quoted in *New York Times*, "Full Document: Trump's Call with the Ukrainian President," October 30, 2019. www.nytimes .com.

11. Quoted in *New York Times*, "Full Document."

12. Quoted in *New York Times*, "Full Document."

13. Quoted in Ed Pilkington and Andrew Roth, "Rudy Giuliani: Ukraine Sources Detail Attempt to Construct Case Against Biden," *The Guardian*, September 29, 2019. www.theguard ian.com.

14. Quoted Polina Ivanova et al., "What Hunter Biden Did on the Board of Ukrainian Energy Company Burisma," Reuters, October 18, 2019. www.reuters.com.

Chapter Two: The House Impeachment Inquiry

15. Quoted in Rebecca Ballhaus, Siobhan Hughes, and Byron Tau, "White House Says It Won't Cooperate with Impeachment Inquiry," *Wall Street Journal*, October 8, 2019, www .wsj.com.

16. Quoted in Charlie Savage and Josh Williams, "Read the Text Messages Between U.S. and Ukrainian Officials," *New York Times*, October 4, 2019. www.nytimes.com.

17. Quoted in Nicholas Fandos, "Why Is Democrats' Impeachment Inquiry Out of Public View," *New York Times*, October 24, 2019. www.nytimes.com.

18. Quoted in BBC News, "White House 'Will Not Co-operate with Impeachment Inquiry,'" October 9, 2019, www.bbc.com.

19. Quoted in Sharon LaFraniere, Nicholas Fandos, and Andrew E. Kramer, "Ukraine Envoy Says She Was Told Trump Wanted Her Out over Lack of Trust," *New York Times*, October 11, 2019. www.nytimes.com.

20. Quoted in Mike Lillis, Rebecca Klar, Olivia Beavers, and Juliegrace Brufke, "Republicans Storm Closed-Door Hearing to

Protest Impeachment Inquiry," *The Hill*, October 23, 2019, www.thehill.com.

21. Quoted in Ephrat Livni, "Republicans Seethe While Suggesting Impeachment-Inquiry Witnesses," Quartz, November 9, 2019. https://qz.com.

22. Quoted in *The Guardian*, "Pelosi Says Trump Is Welcome to Testify in Impeachment Inquiry, If He Chooses," November 17, 2019. www.theguardian.com.

23. Quoted in Madison Dibble, "Vindman Chides Nunes: 'It's Lieutenant Colonel Vindman Please,'" Microsoft News, November 19, 2019. www.msn.com.

24. Quoted in Peter Baker and Michael D. Shear, "Key Moments from the Impeachment Inquiry Hearing: Vindman, Williams, Morrison and Volker Testify," *New York Times*, November 19, 2019. www.nytimes.com.

25. Quoted in Kevin Breuninger, "Trump Ignored Talking Points About 'Corruption' in Zelenskiy Call, Top Security Aide Lt. Col. Alexander Vindman says," CNBC, November 19, 2019. www.cnbc.com.

26. Quoted in Adam Edelman, "7 Things We Learned from Gordon Sondland's Impeachment Testimony," NBC News, November 20, 2019. www.nbcnews.com.

27. Quoted in Nahal Toosi et al., "Impeachment Hearing Grows Heated as GOP Lawmakers Tangle with Witnesses," *Politico*, November 21, 2019. www.politico.com.

Chapter Three: The Impeachment Vote

28. Russell Berman, "The Democrats' Missed Opportunity on Impeachment," *The Atlantic*, December 4, 2019. www.theatlantic.com.

29. Quoted in Adam Liptak, "Key Excerpts from Legal Scholars' Arguments on Impeachment," *New York Times*, December 4, 2019. www.nytimes.com.

30. Quoted in Liptak, "Key Excerpts from Legal Scholars' Arguments on Impeachment."

31. Quoted in Heather Caygle and Sarah Ferris, "'No Choice': Pelosi Proceeds with Articles of Impeachment," *Politico*, December 5, 2019, www.politico.com.

32. Quoted in Siobhan Hughes and Natalie Andrews, "House Democrats Announce Two Articles of Impeachment Against Trump," *Wall Street Journal*, December 10, 2019. www.wsj .com.

33. Quoted in Hughes and Andrews, "House Democrats Announce Two Articles of Impeachment Against Trump."

34. Quoted in Nicholas Fandos and Michael D. Shear, "House Panel Debates Impeachment Articles in Bid to Complete Charges Against Trump," *New York Times*, December 11, 2019. www.nytimes.com.

35. Quoted in Rachael Bade et al., "House Judiciary Committee Abruptly Adjourns After Marathon Debate, Will Vote on Articles of Impeachment Friday Morning," *Washington Post*, December 13, 2019. www.washingtonpost.com.

36. Quoted in Michael Brice-Saddler, John Wagner, and Colby Itkowitz, "House Judiciary Panel Takes Unexpected Recess, Delays Vote on Articles of Impeachment to Friday," *Washington Post*, December 13, 2019. www.washingtonpost.com.

37. Quoted in Jeremy Herb and Manu Raju, "House of Representatives Impeaches President Donald Trump," CNN, December 19, 2019. www.cnn.com.

38. Quoted in Katelyn Burns, "Nancy Pelosi Explains What Democrats Gained by Holding onto the Articles of Impeachment," Vox, January 12, 2020. www.vox.com.

Chapter Four: The Senate Trial

39. Quoted in Seung Min Kim, Felicia Sonmez, and Mike DeBonis, "Senate Adopts Ground Rules for Impeachment Trial, Delaying a Decision on Witnesses Until After Much of the Proceedings," *Washington Post*, January 22, 2020. www .washingtonpost.com.

40. Quoted in Nicholas Fandos, "Republicans Block Subpoenas for New Evidence as Impeachment Trial Begins," *New York Times*, January 21, 2020. www.nytimes.com.

41. Quoted in Fandos, "Republicans Block Subpoenas for New Evidence as Impeachment Trial Begins."

42. Quoted in Jeremy Herb and Manu Raju, "Senate Impeachment Trial: Managers Outline the Case for Removing Trump," CNN, January 23, 2020. www.cnn.com.

43. Quoted in Benjamin Siegel et al., "Trump Impeachment Trial: Democrats Make Case for 'Obstruction of Congress,'" ABC News, January 24, 2020. https://abcnews.go.com.

44. Quoted in Siegel et al., "Trump Impeachment Trial."

45. Quoted in Jonathan Allen, "Trump's Defense Looks Shaky on First Day of Impeachment Trial," NBC News, January 21, 2020. www.nbcnews.com.

46. Quoted in Quinn Owen et al., "Trump Impeachment Trial: President's Defense Team Goes After Bidens," ABC News, January 27, 2020. https://abcnews.go.com.

47. Quoted in Owen et al., "Trump Impeachment Trial."

48. Quoted in Li Zhou, "'Erase All Doubt': Democrats Explain Why John Bolton's Testimony Is So Necessary," Vox, January 29, 2020. www.vox.com.

Chapter Five: Verdict and Aftermath

49. Quoted in Kyle Cheney, Burgess Everett, and Andrew Desiderio, "John Roberts Refuses Rand Paul's Whistleblower Question," *Politico*, January 30, 2020. www.politico.com.

50. Quoted in Grace Segers et al., "Impeachment Trial: First Day of Q&A Session Concludes," CBS News, January 30, 2020. www.cbsnews.com.

51. Quoted in Jennifer Haberkorn et al., "Senate Votes Against Calling Witnesses in Trump Impeachment Trial," *Los Angeles Times*, January 31, 2020. www.latimes.com.

52. Quoted in Haberkorn et al., "Senate Votes Against Calling Witnesses in Trump Impeachment Trial."

53. Quoted in Marc Caputo, "Biden Concedes Iowa Was a 'Gut Punch,'" *Politico*, February 5, 2020. www.politico.com.

54. Quoted in Grace Panetta, "Trump Tweets a Video Implying He'll Be President '4EVA' as His First Official Response After Impeachment-Trial Acquittal," Business Insider, February 5, 2020. www.businessinsider.com.

55. Quoted in *Morning Edition*, "Senate Impeachment Trial Ends: Voters React to Trump's Acquittal," National Public Radio, February 6, 2020. www.npr.org.

56. Charles M. Blow, "They Acquitted Trump. Make Them Pay!," *New York Times*, February 5, 2020. www.nytimes.com.

57. Quoted in *Morning Edition*, "Senate Impeachment Trial Ends."

58. Quoted in Kyle Cheney, Natasha Bertrand, and Meredith McGraw, "Impeachment Witnesses Ousted amid Fears of Trump Revenge Campaign," *Politico*, February 7, 2020. www.politico.com.

59. Quoted in Jeremy Herb, "Trump Fires Intelligence Community Watchdog Who Told Congress About Whistleblower Complaint That Led to Impeachment," CNN, April 4, 2020. www.cnn.com.

60. Andrew Bakaj, John Tye, and Mark Zaid, "Trump's Purge of Inspectors General Is a Crisis. Alarm Bells Should Be Going Off Everywhere," *Washington Post*, April 14, 2020. www.washingtonpost.com.

61. Quoted in Carl Hulse, "With Trump's Trial Over, Lawmakers Ponder How to Conduct the Next One," *New York Times*, February 11, 2020, www.nytimes.com.

Key Figures in the Trump Impeachment

Donald Trump, the US president, was accused of seeking to pressure the Ukrainian government to investigate political rival Joe Biden and his son Hunter. Trump allegedly threatened to withhold military aid from Ukraine.

Volodomyr Zelensky, the president of Ukraine, was allegedly pressured by Trump and his associates to open an investigation into Trump's political rival in exchange for military aid and a White House visit.

Joe Biden, the former vice president, was vying for the Democratic party's presidential nomination during the impeachment proceedings, and eventually became the presumptive nominee.

Hunter Biden, Joe Biden's son, served on the board of Burisma Holdings, an oil and gas company in Ukraine.

The Whistleblower was a CIA officer posted at the White House. This anonymous officer learned about Trump's phone call with the Ukrainian president and filed an official whistleblower complaint.

Michael Atkinson, the inspector general for the US intelligence community, received the whistleblower's complaint, decided it was credible, and passed it along to the House Intelligence Committee.

Joseph Maguire, the acting director of national intelligence, decided the whistleblower's complaint was not urgent, and favored withholding the complaint from Congress.

Nancy Pelosi, a representative from California and the Speaker of the House, launched an inquiry into Trump's alleged abuses in the Ukraine affair.

Adam Schiff, a representative from California and the chairman of the House Intelligence Committee, led the inquiry into the whistleblower's allegations against Trump.

Jerrold Nadler, a representative from New York and the chairman of the House Judiciary Committee, led hearings about Trump's alleged misconduct in the Ukraine affair.

Devin Nunes, a representative from California and the ranking minority party member on the House Intelligence Committee, defended Trump's actions and questioned the basis for the inquiry.

Marie Yovanovitch, the US ambassador to Ukraine, was fired by Trump in May 2019. She alleged that her dismissal came after she refused to support Trump's pressure tactics against Ukraine.

Gordon Sondland, the US ambassador to the European Union, testified that several figures in the administration knew about the attempts to pressure Ukraine into investigating the Bidens.

Alexander Vindman, a lieutenant colonel in the US Army and the top Ukraine specialist on the National Security Council (NSC), testified that it was improper for Trump to demand a foreign investigation of a US citizen.

Fiona Hill, a key adviser on Russia and Ukraine on the NSC, testified that Trump and his associates let domestic politics take precedence over foreign policy in Ukraine.

Mitch McConnell, a Republican senator from Kentucky and the majority leader of the US Senate, led his party in setting the rules for Trump's impeachment trial.

Chuck Schumer, a Democratic senator from New York and the minority leader in the US Senate, coordinated with House managers to present their case against the president in the Senate trial.

Pat Cipollone, the White House counsel, led the legal team defending Trump in the Senate trial.

Mitt Romney, a Republican senator from Utah, voted in favor of removing Trump for obstruction of Congress, becoming the only Republican to do so.

For Further Research

Books

John Bolton, *The Room Where It Happened: A White House Memoir*. New York: Simon & Schuster, 2020 (projected).

Frank O. Bowman III, *High Crimes and Misdemeanors: A History of Impeachment for the Age of Trump*. New York: Cambridge University Press, 2019.

Alan Dershowitz, *The Case Against Impeaching Trump*. New York: Skyhorse, 2019.

Neal Katyal with Sam Koppelman, *Impeach: The Case Against Donald Trump*. New York: Mariner, 2019.

Jon Meacham and the House Intelligence Committee, *The Impeachment Report: The House Intelligence Committee's Report on Its Investigation into Donald Trump and Ukraine*. New York: Broadway, 2019.

Internet Sources

Julian E. Barnes et al., "White House Knew of Whistle-Blower's Allegations Soon After Trump's Call with Ukraine Leader," *New York Times*, September 26, 2019. www.nytimes.com.

Jeremy Herb, "Trump Fires Intelligence Community Watchdog Who Told Congress About Whistleblower Complaint That Led to Impeachment," CNN, April 4, 2020, www.cnn.com.

Siobhan Hughes and Natalie Andrews, "House Democrats Announce Two Articles of Impeachment Against Trump," *Wall Street Journal*, December 10, 2019. www.wsj.com.

Politico, "Read the Trump-Ukraine Phone Call Readout," September 25, 2019. www.politico.com.

Olivia B. Waxman, "Where Trump's Acquittal Fits into the History of Impeachment, According to Historians," *Time*, February 6, 2020. https://time.com.

Li Zhou, "'Erase All Doubt': Democrats Explain Why John Bolton's Testimony Is So Necessary," Vox, January 29, 2020. www.vox .com.

Websites

Brookings Institution (www.brookings.edu). The Brookings Institution is a progressive group devoted to public policy research and education. Its website contains a variety of material about the Trump impeachment, including a podcast titled "What It Means to Impeach a President" and a discussion of what constitutes an impeachable offense.

Hoover Institution (www.hoover.org). The Hoover Institution is a right-of-center think tank based at Stanford University. It has a large archive of articles, editorials, and features about President Trump's impeachment. One comprehensive look at the issues in the case is "The Impeachment Handbook with John Yoo & Richard Epstein."

House Committee on the Judiciary (https://judiciary.house.gov). This official House of Representatives website includes "The Impeachment of Donald John Trump Evidentiary Record from the House of Representatives," which provides documents, reports, and witness transcripts from all the committees involved in the House impeachment inquiry. It offers a comprehensive record of the impeachment proceedings in the House.

ImpeachmentGuide (https://impeachment.guide). The ImpeachmentGuide is a website created by GovTrack.us, a nongovernmental source about the US Congress. The guide contains a wealth of facts and materials about the Trump impeachment, including the charges, a step-by-step chronology, and a history of impeachment.

Vox (www.vox.com). The left-wing political news and analysis website Vox includes the article "Impeachment, Explained: The Ultimate Guide to the Donald Trump Impeachment Saga," which offers a comprehensive look at the impeachment of President Trump. It includes links that explain why Trump was impeached, what his defense was, and the Senate's role in impeachment.

Index

Picture Credits

About the Author

John Allen is a writer who lives in Oklahoma City.